PUFFIN BOOKS

Bless

Blessu

Dick King-Smith

Illustrated by
Adrienne Kennaway

PUFFIN BOOKS

PUFFIN BOOKS

Published by the Penguin Group
Penguin Books Ltd, 27 Wrights Lane, London W8 5TZ, England
Penguin Books USA Inc., 375 Hudson Street, New York, New York 10014, USA
Penguin Books Australia Ltd, Ringwood, Victoria, Australia
Penguin Books Canada Ltd, 10 Alcorn Avenue, Toronto, Ontario, Canada M4V 3B2
Penguin Books (NZ) Ltd, 182–190 Wairau Road, Auckland 10, New Zealand

Penguin Books Ltd, Registered Offices: Harmondsworth, Middlesex, England

First published by Hamish Hamilton 1990
Published in Puffin Books 1995
9 10

Text copyright © Fox Busters Ltd, 1990
Illustrations copyright © Adrienne Kennaway, 1990
All rights reserved

The moral right of the author and illustrator has been asserted

Made and printed in Belgium by Proost

Blessu was a very small elephant when he
sneezed for the first time.

The herd was moving slowly through the tall elephant-grass, so tall that it hid the legs of his mother and his aunties, and reached halfway up the bodies of his bigger brothers and sisters.

But you couldn't see Blessu at all.

Down below, where he was walking, the air was thick with pollen from the flowering elephant-grasses, and suddenly Blessu felt a strange tickly feeling at the base of his very small trunk.

Shutting his eyes and closing his mouth, he stuck his very small trunk straight out before him, and sneezed:

"AAARCHOOO!"

It wasn't the biggest sneeze in the world, but it was very big for a very small elephant.

"BLESS YOU!"

cried his mother and his aunties and his
bigger brothers and sisters.

For a moment Blessu looked rather cowed. He did not know what they meant, and he thought he might have done something naughty. He hung his head and his ears drooped.

But the herd moved on through the tall elephant-grass without taking any further notice of him, so he soon forgot to be unhappy.

Before long Blessu gave another sneeze, and another, and another, and each time he sneezed, his mother and his aunties and his bigger brothers and sisters cried:

"BLESS YOU!"

They did not say this to any of the other
elephants, Blessu noticed (because none of
the other elephants sneezed), so he
thought, 'That must be my name.'

At last the herd came out of the tall elephant-grass and went down to the river, to drink and to bathe, and Blessu stopped sneezing.

"Poor baby!" said his mother, touching the top of his hairy little head gently with the tip of her trunk. "You've got awful hay-fever."

"And what a sneeze he's got!" said one of his aunties. "It's not the biggest sneeze in the world, but it's very big for a very small elephant."

The months passed, and Blessu grew,
very slowly, as elephants do. But so did
his hay-fever. Worse and worse it got and
more and more he sneezed as the herd
moved through the tall elephant-grass.

Every few minutes Blessu would shut
his eyes and close his mouth and stick his
very small trunk straight out before him
and sneeze:

"AAAARCHOOOO!!"

And each time he sneezed, his mother and his aunties and his bigger brothers and sisters cried:

"BLESS YOU!"

But though Blessu was not growing very fast, one bit of him was.

It was his trunk. All that sneezing was stretching it.

Soon he had to carry it tightly curled up, so as not to trip on it.

"Poor baby!" said his mother. "At this rate your trunk will soon be as long as mine."

But Blessu only answered:

"AAAARCHOOOO!!"

"Don't worry, my dear," said one of his aunties. "The longer the better, I should think. He'll be able to reach higher up into the trees than any elephant ever has, and he'll be able to go deeper into the river (using his trunk as a snorkel)."

"Ah well," said Blessu's mother. "Soon the elephant-grass will finish flowering, and the poor little chap will stop sneezing."

And it did.

And he did.

The years passed, and each year brought
the season of the flowering of the elephant-
grasses, that shed their pollen and made
Blessu sneeze.

And each sneeze stretched that trunk of
his just a little bit further.

By the time he was five years old, he
could reach as high into the trees, and go
as deep into the river (using his trunk as a
snorkel) as his mother and his aunties.

By the time he was ten years old, he could reach higher and go deeper.

And by the time Blessu was twenty years old, and had grown a fine pair of tusks, he had, without doubt, the longest trunk of any elephant in the whole of Africa.

And now, in the season of the flowering of the elephant-grasses, what a sneeze he had!

Shutting his eyes and closing his mouth, he stuck his amazingly long trunk straight out before him and sneezed:

"AAAAAARCHOOOOOOO!!!"

Woe betide anything that got in the way of that sneeze!

Young trees were uprooted, birds were
blown whirling into the sky, small animals
like antelope and gazelle were bowled over
and over, larger creatures such as zebra
and wildebeest stampeded in panic before
that mighty blast, and even the King of
Beasts took care to be out of the line of fire
of the biggest sneeze in the world.

So if ever you should be in Africa when the elephant-grass is in flower, and should chance to see a great tusker with the longest trunk you could possibly imagine – keep well away, and watch, and listen.

You will see that great tusker shut his eyes and close his mouth and stick his fantastically, unbelievably, impossibly long trunk straight out before him. And you will hear:

"AAAAAARCHOOOOOO!!!"

And then you know what to say, don't you?

"BLESSU!"

DUMPLING
Dick King-Smith

Dumpling wishes she could be long and sausage-shaped like other dachshunds. When a witch's cat grants her wish Dumpling becomes the longest dog ever.

SOS FOR RITA
Hilda Offen

Rita is the youngest in her family and her older brothers and sister give her the most boring things to do. What they don't know is that Rita has another identity: she is also the fabulous Rita the Rescuer!

WHAT STELLA SAW
Wendy Smith

Stella's mum is a fortune teller who always gets things wrong. But when football-mad Stella starts reading tea-leaves, she seems to be right every time! Or is she . . .